GW01090706

The March of Time

Contents

The Educational Company

AN
AGE OF REVOLUTION

The transport revolution: the first train arrives in Macroom

■ FACT FILE

The 18th century (1700-1799)

The 18th century was a time of revolution. Various types of revolution were taking place:

1 A **political revolution** changed the way countries were run.
2 A **social revolution** changed the way people lived.
3 An **agricultural revolution** changed the way in which food was grown.
4 An **industrial revolution** changed the way in which goods were made.
5 A **transport revolution** changed the way in which goods and people were carried from one place to another.

Reason for the industrial revolution

Many agree that the enormous growth of population in Europe contributed to the industrial revolution.
This graph shows the growth of population in Ireland and Britain between 1740 and 1840.

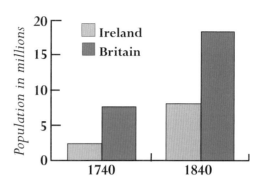

Reasons for the political revolutions

Absolute monarchy/total power

In the 18th century most countries in Europe were ruled by monarchs, i.e. kings, queens, emperors or empresses. They were called 'absolute monarchs' because they had total power and could do as they wished.

An exception was Britain, where **King George III** (3rd) was bound by the decisions of the parliament.

Writers

Writers like **John Locke**, an Englishman, and two Frenchmen, **Voltaire** and **Rousseau,** criticised those monarchs and the old ways of ruling nations.

John Locke   *Voltaire*   *Jean Jacques Rousseau*

3

As a result people questioned many beliefs that had been widely held, and they wondered about the best way to govern a country. The work of those writers weakened people's belief in absolute monarchy or total power and prepared the way for revolutions in America, France and Ireland.

■ THINK AND WRITE

1 Why was the middle and late 18th century often referred to as the era of revolutions? _____

_____

2 Name three countries in which revolutions took place. _____

_____

3 What changed as a result of the industrial revolution? _____

_____

4 Give one reason for the industrial revolution. _____

_____

5 What is meant by 'absolute monarchs'? _____

_____

6 Name two writers who inspired people to question how they were ruled.

_____

7 What growth in population did Ireland have between 1740 and 1840?

_____

8 Why, in your opinion, did population growth contribute to the industrial revolution? _____

_____

■ EXERCISE

Old ways

The picture shows farming in France in the 18th century – before the agricultural revolution.

List five differences between farming in the picture and farming today.

IRELAND DURING THE REVOLUTION ERA

A typical labourer's cottage of the 18th century

■ FACT FILE

Late 18th century Ireland

80% of Irish people lived in the country and worked on the land.

The land belonged mainly to about 20,000 landlords. Most of the Irish farmers had little land and were very poor. Cottiers and labourers had no land and most of them lived in great poverty. 'Spailpíns' were labourers who travelled from county to county, working for farmers.

A labourer might earn 6 pence (2.5p) a day and a meal. Meals consisted mainly of dry potatoes and maybe a cup of buttermilk. The labourer's cabin was made of mud or clay walls and was thatched. A pig was often kept in the house.

A spailpín

Cost of clothing

	Coat	Trousers	Shirt	Apron	Cap	Socks
Mid–18th century	85p	38p	10p	5p	2p	5p
Now	£120	£40	£10	£4	£8	£3

Table comparing the cost of clothes today with cost in mid-18th century

■ THINK AND WRITE

1 Who owned most of the land in Ireland in the late 18th century? _____
_____

2 Where did most of the population live? _____
_____

3 Why did they live mainly in the country? _____
_____

4 What kind of houses did the majority of labourers have? _____
_____

5 Who were 'spailpíns'? _____
_____

6 What was the main diet of the poorer people? _____
_____

■ EXERCISE

The picture below shows the house of a strong farmer.

Write three sentences about the differences between this house
and the one on page 6.

THE AMERICAN REVOLUTION: 1776

■ FACT FILE

4 Canada and a part of southern America called Louisiana belonged to the French.

2 People from northern Europe settled on the east coast. They came from Britain and Ireland, as well as from France and Germany. Many were seeking religious freedom.

1 Before the Europeans came, the American continent was the home of native American tribes. Columbus had called them 'Indians'. Those who lived near the coast were farmers and fishermen. Natives who lived on the great plains hunted the vast herds of deer and buffalo.

3 In Britain's southern colonies, black Africans were used as slaves. They worked on large farms called plantations, where their masters became rich by growing rice, sugar and tobacco. Many of these wealthy men were among the leaders of the American Revolution.

5 Spain claimed the rest of North America, but few people settled in this region. Europeans knew little about the native people of this area.

Map of America showing areas settled by Europeans

Causes of the American Revolution

By the mid-18th century millions of Europeans went to America to seek their fortunes and to find religious freedom.

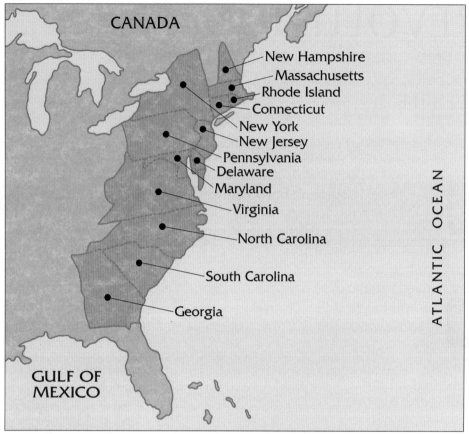

Map of American east coast showing the thirteen colonies ruled by Britain

Britain ruled thirteen colonies on the east coast of America.

The Americans were very annoyed at the trade restrictions and taxes imposed on them by Britain:

1 Americans could sell tobacco or rice only to Britain.
2 Americans had to buy sugar from British colonies.
3 Americans could not start an iron industry.
4 Americans had to pay new taxes called stamp duties, e.g. for every pack of playing cards, 5p (one shilling) had to be paid. For newspapers and for every legal document, stamp duty had also to be paid.
5 The Americans had no votes in the British parliament. They summed up their viewpoint in the slogan '**no taxation without representation**'.

The Boston Tea Party

In 1773 a row blew up as tea was brought in from India, and Americans had to pay tax on it. When the ships carrying the tea entered Boston harbour, a mob disguised as Indians went on board and dumped the tea into the harbour. This is referred to as the 'Boston Tea Party'.

Tea being dumped from a ship in Boston harbour

The first Congress

In 1774 a congress (coming together) of delegates from the thirteen colonies met in Philadelphia. They set down the colonists' right to life, liberty, and property. They decided to take up arms to defend themselves. Their fighting men were known as 'Minutemen' because they were ready to march at a minute's notice.

The American War of Independence: 1775-1781

The British army was experienced but was over 3,000 miles from home. The Americans were inexperienced but had the support of the people and a great leader in **George Washington**.

The first battle of the war was the Battle of Lexington where the British destroyed American guns. The following day the Battle of Concord was fought. The American War of Independence had begun.

The ambush of the British forces at Lexington

■ THINK AND WRITE

1 Name five types of revolution which took place in the 18th century.

_____

_____

2 Write a sentence about any two types of 18th century revolution.

_____

_____

3 Study the graph on page 3 and write down the approximate increase in the population of Ireland between 1740 and 1840. _____

_____

4 What form of government did most European countries have in the 18th century?_____

5 Name three famous writers who lived during the 18th century.

_____

6 What type of work were the majority of Irish people engaged in during the 18th century? _____

_____

7 Who were called spailpíns? _____

_____

8 Of what materials were the majority of labourers' cabins made?

_____

9   Name a domestic animal that was sometimes kept in a cabin.

_____

10   What would be the total cost of a shirt, coat, and socks in the 18th century?_____

11   Mention two trade restrictions placed on the Americans by the British.

_____

12 Study the maps on pages 9 and 10 and write down the names of the main colonies in which Irish emigrants settled. _____

_____

_____

13   In 1773 the Americans did not want to pay tax on tea imported from India. (a) What happened as a result? _____

_____

(b) Where did the event take place? _____

(c) How were the attackers of the ship disguised?_____

14 What war was fought from 1775 to 1781?_____

_____

15 Who was the great American leader at the time of the War of Independence? _____

■ A BALLAD

In April 1775 a courier named Paul Revere rode through the night to warn the Minutemen of the state of Massachusetts about the movement of British troops. The event was celebrated in a ballad by the poet H.W. Longfellow. Here are some extracts from the ballad.

Paul Revere's Ride

Listen, my children, and you shall hear
Of the midnight ride of Paul Revere,
On the eighteenth of April, in Seventy-five;
Hardly a man is now alive
Who remembers that famous day and year.

He said to his friend, 'If the British march
By land or sea from the town to-night,
Hang a lantern aloft in the belfry arch
Of the North Church tower as a signal light, -
One, if by land, and two, if by sea;
And I on the opposite shore will be,
Ready to ride and spread the alarm
Through every Middlesex village and farm,
For the country folk to be up and to arm.'

        . . . . .

But mostly he watched with eager search
The belfry-tower of the Old North Church,
As it rose above the graves on the hill,
Lonely and spectral and sombre and still.
And lo! as he looks, on the belfry's height
A glimmer, and then a gleam of light!
He springs to the saddle, the bridle he turns,
But lingers and gazes, till full on his sight
A second lamp in the belfry burns!

It was twelve by the village clock
When he crossed the bridge into Medford town.
He heard the crowing of the cock,
And the barking of the farmer's dog,
And felt the damp of the river fog,
That rises after the sun goes down.

It was one by the village clock
When he galloped into Lexington.
He saw the gilded weathercock
Swim in the moonlight as he passed,
And the meeting-house windows, blank and bare,
Gaze at him with a spectral glare,
As if they already stood aghast
At the bloody work they would look upon.

It was two by the village clock
When he came to the bridge in Concord town.
He heard the bleating of the flock,
And the twitter of birds among the trees,
And felt the breath of the morning breeze
Blowing over the meadows brown.
And one was safe and asleep in his bed
Who at the bridge would be first to fall.
Who that day would be lying dead,
Pierced by a British musket ball.

You know the rest. In the books you have read
How the British regulars fired and fled,
How the farmers gave them ball for ball,
From behind each fence and farmyard wall,
Chasing the red-coats down the lane,
Then crossing the fields to emerge again
Under the trees at the turn of the road
And only pausing to fire and load.
. . . . .
For, borne on a night-wind of the Past,
Through all our history, to the last,
In the hour of darkness and peril and need,
The people will waken and listen to hear
The hurrying hoof-beats of that steed,
And the midnight message of Paul Revere.

■ GLEANINGS

If we read the ballad carefully, we can get some information about the place and the time in which the event took place. What does the ballad suggest to you about

(a) methods of communication at the time
(b) the type of people who fought on the American side
(c) any advantage the local Minutemen had over the British forces
(d) the method of fighting employed by the American force
(e) the way of life of the people in and near Lexington and Concord?
(f) What is suggested by the final five lines of the ballad?

■ FACT FILE

Declaration of Independence: 4 July 1776

The Declaration of Independence was written by Thomas Jefferson and was passed by Congress on 4 July 1776.

Issuing the Declaration of Independence on 4 July 1776

Result of the American Revolution

The Americans set up a form of government known as a republic. They formed the United States of America. George Washington became the first president of the USA in 1789.

The Americans then drew up a **Bill of Rights**. It guaranteed to all citizens

- the right to life
- the right to liberty
- the right to free speech
- the right to practise the religion of their choice
- the right to pursuit of happiness.

A constitution (a set of principles and rules for governing the country) was drawn up, and it is still in operation today.

■ EXERCISE

Write the names of the thirteen original British colonies in the map below. (They correspond to today's states of the same names.) Check their position in your atlas.

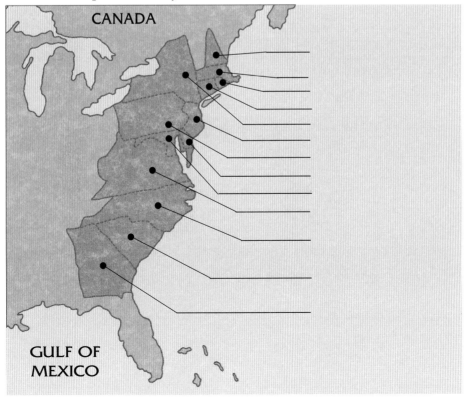

■ THINK AND WRITE

1 Name the thirteen colonies ruled by Britain in America. _____

_____

_____

_____

2 On which coast of America were the colonies situated? _____

_____

3 Name two trade restrictions that annoyed the Americans. _____

_____

4 What was the name of the tax which had to be paid for legal
documents? _____

5 What slogan did the Americans adopt in relation to being taxed and
not having a vote? _____

6 What 'party' took place in 1773? _____

7 How long did the American War of Independence last? _____

_____

8 What will Thomas Jefferson be remembered for? _____

_____

9 In what year was the Declaration of Independence made? _____

_____

10 What form of government was set up as a result of the Declaration
of Independence? _____

_____

11 Name three rights included in the Bill of Rights. _____

_____

12 Name the first president of the USA. _____

_____

18

THE FRENCH REVOLUTION: 1789

■ FACT FILE

People in Europe, especially in France and Ireland, took a great interest in the American Revolution. France gave supplies and money to the Americans to help them in the war against Britain, and many French soldiers served on the American side.

The American Revolution affected France in two special ways:

1 The success of the Americans against Britain and George III (3rd) encouraged the French people to rebel against King Louis XVI (16th) and to attempt to gain control of government.
2 France became bankrupt for its part in the American War of Independence. King Louis failed to get the people's representatives to help him raise new taxes.

The French Revolution

The French people were heavily taxed, had few rights and were poor. King Louis XVI and Queen Marie Antoinette lived in great luxury in the palace at Versailles.

A meeting of the Estates General (the old French parliament) was held on 5 May 1789. There were three groups in the Estates General:

1 The First Estate, representing the clergy
2 The Second Estate, representing the nobility
3 The Third Estate, representing everyone else, e.g. workers, business people, professionals etc.

Up to then the nobility and clergy had controlled parliament, but now the Third Estate declared that they were in control of the National Assembly.

The attack on the Bastille

Rumours spread around Paris that King Louis was going to close down the Assembly. On 14 July 1789, the citizens of Paris attacked and captured the Bastille, a prison where arms and ammunition were stored. The French Revolution had begun.

During the revolution thousands of nobles, including the king and queen, were put to death at the guillotine.

The execution of King Louis XVI

Results of the French Revolution

1 A new form of government known as a republic was set up in France.
2 All unfair taxes and privileges of the nobility were removed.
3 Many reforms were introduced, e.g. the Declaration of the Rights of Man.
4 Slavery was abolished in all lands belonging to France.
5 The metric system in use today was introduced.
6 The French Revolution became an inspiration to other countries, especially Ireland.

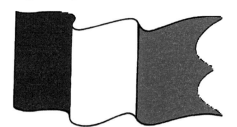

Liberty
Equality
Fraternity

The flag and the motto of the French revolutionaries

■ THINK AND WRITE

1 State one way in which the American Revolution influenced the French Revolution. _____

2 Were the ordinary people of France happy to see the king and queen live in great luxury? _____

3 Who were represented in the Estates General (the old French parliament)? _____

4 What group represented the workers? _____

5 Who were king and queen of France at the time of the revolution?

_____

6 What action began the French Revolution? _____

_____

7 What was the main method of execution used during the revolution?

_____

■ EXERCISES

1 Put words from the box in the spaces.

world	Americans	Equality	republic	taxed
stored	Fraternity	Louis XVI	Bastille	Versailles
taxes	America	Marie Antoinette		

Many Frenchmen fought on the side of the _____ in the American War of Independence. When they returned to France, they brought news of freedom and civil rights won by the people of _____. In France the people were heavily _____. But the nobles did not pay _____. King _____ _____ and Queen _____ _____ lived in luxury in their palace at _____.
On 14 July 1789 the people of Paris attacked the _____. Arms and ammunition were _____ there. The revolution had begun, and soon it spread to the countryside.
The motto of the revolutionaries was 'Liberty, _____, _____. In 1792 France was declared a _____. The revolutions in France and America had a lasting effect all over the _____.

2 This cartoon and caption appeared at the time of the French Revolution. The characters represent the Estates General.

Write what you think is the point made by the cartoon.

Let's hope that this will all be over soon

22

THE IRISH REBELLION: 1798

■ FACT FILE

In the 18th century the Irish were unhappy at the way they were governed, just as the Americans and French had been. Ireland had its own parliament but yet it was under the control of the British government.

The power of the Irish parliament was severely limited by

1 **Poynings' Law:** The Irish parliament could not meet without the permission of the king of England, and all laws passed by it had to get the approval of the king and his council in England.
2 **The Sixth Act of George I:** An act passed by the British parliament granting to itself the power to make laws governing Ireland.

Penal Laws were a number of anti-Catholic laws, passed in the 18th century. Those laws placed severe restrictions on Catholics, the majority of whom lived in poverty.

While Britain was involved in the American War of Independence, members of the Irish parliament, under **Henry Grattan**, succeeded in having Poynings' Law and the Sixth Act of George I repealed.

■ PEN PORTRAIT

Henry Grattan

- A lawyer by profession
- Member of the Irish parliament from 1775
- A great orator
- Leader of the Patriot Party
- The Irish parliament became known as 'Grattan's parliament'.

Henry Grattan stands to speak in the Irish parliament

■ FACT FILE

French Revolution welcomed in Ireland

In 1789, people in Ireland heard the news about the French Revolution. Many people were pleased with the news. One of them was **Theobald Wolfe Tone**, a young Dublin lawyer. He believed that Irish people, too, should be free.

Wolfe Tone

Wolfe Tone was born in Dublin in 1763. He was a Protestant who was educated in Dublin and London. The motto of the French Revolution, 'Liberty, Equality, Fraternity', appealed to Wolfe Tone.

Wolfe Tone

The Society of the United Irishmen

In 1791, Tone went to Belfast where he met some Presbyterians who also admired the French Revolution. They formed the **Society of United Irishmen**. The society adopted three of Tone's resolutions:

1 People must unite against repression to protect their liberties and develop trade.
2 The method of electing MPs must be changed so that they represent more of the people.
3 Reform is not just if it does not include people of every religion.

The aim of the society was to unite Irish people of all religions and, by peaceful means, to win liberty and equality. The United Irishmen spread throughout the country. Lord Edward Fitzgerald became one of their leaders in Dublin.

Britain went to war with France in 1793, and the United Irishmen were banned.

■ THINK AND WRITE

1 When did the French Revolution occur? _____

2 What was the motto of the French Revolution?_____

   _____

3 Where was Wolfe Tone born? _____

4 Why were the United Irishmen formed? _____

   _____

5 Why, in your opinion, did Britain ban the United Irishmen? _____

   _____

■ EXERCISES

1   Draw a banner with the words 'Liberty, Equality, Fraternity'.
    Colour the letters in the colours of the French flag
    (blue, white, red).

2   Use your dictionary to help you to find out the exact meaning
    of the words

           Liberty   Equality   Fraternity.

3   Make up a motto for your class. Draw a banner for your motto.

4   Write two sentences about each of the men in the pictures.

■ FACT FILE

Wolfe Tone goes to France

In 1794 Wolfe Tone went to France to seek help for a revolution in Ireland. On 15 December 1796, 43 ships carrying 15,000 soldiers sailed from France to Ireland. Tone was on one of the ships.

Storm at sea

French ships in stormy waters in Bantry Bay, December 1796

The French ships ran into fierce storms. Many were blown off course and never reached Ireland. On 21 December, Tone's ship sailed into Bantry Bay in County Cork. Only fourteen ships out of the 43 managed to get to Bantry Bay. They stayed for six days in the bay without being able to land because of the bad weather. On 29 December 1796 the French ships decided to return to France. Tone returned to France with the fleet.

The search for weapons

Word soon spread of the attempt to land French soldiers in Bantry Bay. The British sent an army to Ulster to search for weapons. Then the army was sent into Leinster. People were tortured to make them say where weapons were hidden. The United Irishmen leaders knew they must begin the rebellion before all the weapons were gone.

Cartoon of Captain Swayne pitch-capping a peasant. (A 'cap' filled with boiling pitch was placed on the person's head.) Swayne was commander of the soldiers in Wexford.

■ THINK AND WRITE

1 Why did Wolfe Tone go to France? _____

_____

2 How many ships sailed from France to Ireland? _____

3 How many got as far as Bantry Bay? _____

4 How long did the ships stay in Bantry Bay? _____

5 How many soldiers sailed from France? _____

6 During what season did the ships sail? _____

7 Why was there a big search for weapons during 1797? _____

_____

8 What decision did the leaders of the United Irishmen take? _____

_____

■ EXERCISES

1 Imagine you are Wolfe Tone on board a French ship in Bantry Bay. A storm is raging outside. The soldiers cannot get to land. Write a diary for day 1 and day 6 of the six days.
2 Draw a picture of the French ships returning to France. Write an account of what happened.

■ FACT FILE

The 1798 rebellion

The rebellion began in Leinster. The government had plenty of warning, and the rebels were easily defeated in Kildare and Carlow.

In Wexford soldiers had been ill-treating the people. Father Murphy of Boolavogue was angry. When the soldiers burned the church at Boolavogue, he decided to lead the people in rebellion. The rebels were armed with home-made pikes and farm tools. They defeated the militia at Oulart, and then took Enniscorthy and Wexford. They then attacked but failed to capture New Ross and were finally defeated.

A pikeman of 1798

Vinegar Hill

The rebels were driven from New Ross and retreated to Vinegar Hill, near Enniscorthy. They numbered about 20,000 in total. The government sent an army against them. Many rebels were killed. The rebellion in Wexford was over.

■ A POEM

Requiem for the Croppies

The pockets of our great coats full of barley —
No kitchens on the run, no striking camp —
We moved quick and sudden in our own country.
The priest lay behind ditches with the tramp.
A people, hardly marching — on the hike —
We found new tactics happening each day:
We'd cut through reins and rider with the pike
And stampede cattle into infantry,
Then retreat through hedges where cavalry must be thrown.
Until, on Vinegar Hill, the fatal conclave.
Terraced thousands died, shaking scythes at cannon.
The hillside blushed, soaked in our broken wave.
They buried us without shroud or coffin
And in August the barley grew up out of the grave.

Seamus Heaney

Seamus Heaney received the Nobel Prize for Literature in 1995.

■ GLEANINGS

(a) Who were the Croppies?
(b) Do you think the Croppies had a well-prepared battle plan?
     Write one line from the poem which gives the answer.
(c) What weapons did the Croppies have?
(d) What, do you think, is meant by the phrase, 'the hillside
     blushed'?
(e) Although the Croppies were defeated, and many of them were
     killed, the spirit of revolution lived on among the people.
     How does the poem hint at this?
(f) Illustrate a scene from the poem and give your picture a title.

FACT FILE

Help from France

Wolfe Tone was still in France at the time of the rebellions in Leinster and Ulster. After many attempts he persuaded the French to send another army to Ireland. In August 1798 about 1,000 French troops landed in Killala Bay in County Mayo.

The 'Races of Castlebar'

The people of the west welcomed the French. From all over Connaught they flocked to join them. General Humbert, the French leader, marched to Castlebar, where a small garrison of British troops were stationed. The garrison abandoned their guns and ran away. This became known as the 'Races of Castlebar'.

More French troops come to Ireland

The British sent a large army to Connaught and they defeated General Humbert's troops. Some weeks later a number of French ships carrying reinforcements came to Ireland. This time they arrived in Lough Swilly in County Donegal. Wolfe Tone was aboard one of the ships.

However, British ships were waiting for them. They defeated the French and prevented them from coming ashore.

Death of Wolfe Tone

Wolfe Tone was captured and imprisoned in Dublin. He was sentenced to be hanged on 12 November. But before the sentence could be carried out, he was found dead in his cell. He is buried in Bodenstown in County Kildare.

The rebellion of 1798 was then over. About 30,000 people had been killed and many more had suffered greatly.

■ THINK AND WRITE

1 What happened at Vinegar Hill? _____

_____

2 What part did Wolfe Tone play in the 1798 rebellion? _____

_____

3 What happened at Killala Bay? _____

_____

4 Who was General Humbert? _____

_____

5 What happened at Lough Swilly? _____

_____

6 Why did the British not want the French to succeed in Ireland?

_____

_____

7 Why, do you think, did France, and not some other European
   country, send troops to Ireland? _____

_____

8 Where did Wolfe Tone die? _____

_____

9 Where is he buried? _____

_____

■ EXERCISES

1 Write the appropriate caption in each box, and mark and name the following towns and cities: Wexford, Dublin, Belfast, Cork.

Captions:

Bantry Bay:	French fleet tried to land in 1796.
Belfast:	United Irishmen were founded in 1791.
Killala Bay:	One thousand French troops landed in 1798.
Lough Swilly:	French fleet tried to land in October 1798.
Vinegar Hill:	Battle of the 1798 rebellion.
Bodenstown:	Wolfe Tone is buried here.

2 Put words from the box in the spaces.

Wexford	poorly	peasants	rebelled	Most
rulers	revolutions	hanged	rebels	church
capture	defeated	army	John Murphy	

The success of the _____ in America and France was encouraging for oppressed people all over the world. People saw that it was possible to overthrow _____ who mistreated them.

_____ of the Irish people at that time had harder lives than the French peasants who _____ in 1789. Small groups of _____ staged rebellions in Counties Kildare, Carlow, and Wicklow. They were _____ organised and they were easily defeated.

Only in _____ did the 1798 rebellion meet with any success. The troops sent to Wexford to search for weapons were members of the North Cork Militia. When they burned the _____ at Boolavogue, the parish curate, Fr _____ _____, led his people against the army. Armed with pikes, scythes, and pitch-forks for the most part, the people _____ the militia at Oulart. They went on to _____ Enniscorthy and Wexford. A large government _____, led by General Lake, defeated the _____ at Vinegar Hill. Father Murphy was captured and _____ at Tullow, County Carlow.

■ A BALLAD

Boolavogue

At Boolavogue, as the sun was setting
O'er the bright May meadows of Shelmalier
A rebel hand set the heather blazing
And brought the neighbours from far and near.
Then Father Murphy from old Kilcormack
Spurred up the rocks with a warning cry:
'Arm, Arm!' he cried, 'for I've come to lead you
For Ireland's freedom we fight or die'...

We took Camolin and Enniscorthy,
And Wexford storming, drove out our foes;
'Twas at Slieve Coillte our pikes were reeking
With the crimson stream of the beaten Yeos.
At Tubberneering and Ballyellis
Full many a Hessian lay in his gore;
Ah, Father Murphy, had aid come over,
The green flag floated from shore to shore.

At Vinegar Hill, o'er the pleasant Slaney,
Our heroes vainly stood back to back,
And the Yeos at Tullow took Father Murphy
And burned his body upon the rack.
God grant you glory, brave Father Murphy,
And open Heaven to all your men;
The cause that called you may call tomorrow
In another fight for the Green again.

P. J. McCall

■ GLEANINGS

(a) Who is the hero of this ballad?
(b) What was the signal for the people to take to arms?
(c) What would have happened, according to the balladeer, if the Wexford rebels had got help?
(d) Write the line which suggests that the rebels were surrounded on Vinegar Hill.
(e) What link is there between the final two lines of this ballad and the final line of the poem *Requiem for the Croppies* by Seamus Heaney?

Father Murphy at Boolavogue calling on the people to fight

■ FACT FILE

The rising in Ulster

The Wexford rising was not organised by the United Irishmen. It was a spontaneous outburst against the cruelty of the military. In Ulster the United Irishmen had been waiting for help from France, though some of the younger members, such as Henry Joy McCracken, were impatient. The events in Wexford, however, forced their hands.

Down and Antrim were chosen as the battlefields and the leaders hoped that the rising would spread to the rest of Ulster. This did not happen.

On 7 June 1798 McCracken led an army of about 4,000 men against Antrim town. The authorities knew of the plan beforehand through the treachery of an informer and McCracken and his army were defeated. The rebels were offered an amnesty on condition that they hand up their arms and release prisoners. They accepted the terms and the rising in Antrim was over.

In Down Henry Munroe tried to capture Ballinahinch, but his army of 7,000 men was overwhelmed.

The two leaders were hanged, but their followers were set free.

■ EXERCISE

Thomas Robinson, who lived near the scene of the battle, painted this picture of the Battle of Ballinahinch. Write three sentences about the picture.

■ FACT FILE

The Act of Union

Many people in Britain were frightened by the 1798 rebellion. They were afraid that more French troops could be sent to Ireland. They decided to bind Ireland more closely to Britain. The best way to do this was to unite the two countries under one parliament. In 1800 the Act of Union was passed. This act abolished the separate Irish parliament. From 1800 until 1922 Ireland was ruled directly from Britain.

The Irish House of Parliament in College Green, Dublin. Built in 1739, it was sold to the Bank of Ireland after the Act of Union in 1800

■ THINK AND WRITE

1 What happened in 1800? _____

_____

2 Why was the Act of Union passed? _____

_____

WORD SEARCH

T	H	E	B	O	M	U	N	R	O	E	L
R	E	V	O	L	U	T	I	O	N	D	S
W	E	X	F	O	R	D	U	N	O	F	T
F	R	E	B	E	P	D	O	M	G	R	O
E	W	W	A	S	H	I	N	G	T	O	N
D	A	R	S	K	Y	E	N	E	A	D	E
A	T	R	T	O	S	S	A	N	X	D	S
P	A	R	I	S	E	T	B	Y	T	H	E
S	L	A	L	I	B	E	R	T	Y	N	E
Y	O	U	L	A	R	T	S	R	E	D	W
A	P	R	E	S	I	D	E	N	T	V	E

Words answering to the clues below are hidden in this word puzzle.
They can be read across or down. Cross out the words. The letters
which remain give two lines from a 1798 ballad. Write those lines.

Across
1 A leader of the rising in Ulster
2 A county in the south-east of Ireland
3 Rebellion
4 Freedom
5 An American president
6 American head of state
7 A city in France
8 Battlefield in Wexford

Down
1 Captured at the start of the French Revolution
2 Name of a rebel priest
3 Money paid to government
4 He is buried in Bodenstown.

The hidden lines:

_____

_____

_____

1 What is a social revolution?
2 What was the population of Ireland around 1840?
3 In what way did writers like Voltaire, Locke and Rousseau affect people's views?
4 Could King George III be termed an 'absolute monarch'?
5 What countries influenced the rebellion of 1798 in Ireland?
6 How many colonies did Britain rule in America?
7 Name two of the trade restrictions that annoyed the Americans.
8 Name the slogan used by the Americans when they were denied a vote and were expected to pay extra taxes.
9 In 1773 a row blew up in Boston harbour. It is often referred to as ___ _____ ___ _____.
10 In the War of Independence, the Americans were less experienced but had one major advantage. Name the advantage.
11 What form of government was formed in America after the American Revolution?
12 When do Americans celebrate Independence Day?
13 Who wrote the Declaration of Independence?
14 Who was the first president of the USA?
15 King Louis XVI's wife was called _____ _____.
16 Who did the Third Estate represent?
17 What famous prison in France was attacked at the start of the French Revolution?
18 How were people executed during the French Revolution?
19 What form of government was set up after the French Revolution?
20 Who wrote the three resolutions adopted by the United Irishmen?
21 In what county was Fr Murphy a curate?
22 At what battle was he finally defeated?
23 How did Father John Murphy die?
24 What weapons were used by the rebels in Wexford?

THE
AGE OF O'CONNELL

■ FACT FILE

Daniel O'Connell

Daniel O'Connell was born near Cahirciveen in
County Kerry in 1775. He was sent to his uncle
in Derrynane to be reared.

His first school was a hedge school. Later he was
sent to a school in Cork. He studied law in France
and became a successful lawyer. He defended many
Catholics tried under the Penal Laws.

Daniel O'Connell

O'Connell took up the fight for Catholic emancipation
(the removal of the Penal Laws against Catholics).
He organised the Catholic rent, a system of collecting funds to
fight for emancipation. He spoke at meetings in many parts of the
country, and thousands flocked to listen to him.

O'Connell's home, Derrynane Abbey, County Kerry

During the early part of the 19th century Daniel O'Connell was the most important man in Ireland. He was in France at the time of the revolution and witnessed great violence and bloodshed. As a lawyer he was famous for his powerful speaking voice and sharp brain.

In 1823 O'Connell and some of his friends in the law profession founded the Catholic Association to win Catholic emancipation for the Catholic people of Ireland.

Clare Election: 1828

In 1828 a by-election was held in Clare. A local landlord, Vesey Fitzgerald, was seeking election and was expected to be unopposed, but O'Connell was put forward as a candidate, and there was great excitement.

■ A NEWSPAPER REPORT

A reporter from the *Freeman's Journal* newspaper described the scene in Ennis on the opening day.

8 o'clock a.m: Between 300 and 400 voters are now passing up the streets to the Courthouse, preceded by colours, everyone having a green leaf in his hat. Along the road the general cry of these men was 'Here's Kilrush; High for O'Connell; High for our priest.' Mr O'Leary, the priest of Kilrush, is with them and the town is full of Catholic clergy.
There are fifteen booths open for polling.
10 o'clock: Mr M'Inerney, the priest of Feakle, is just passing at the head of a number of voters from that parish, carrying green boughs and music before them.
11 o'clock: Another large body of men has passed preceded by a green silk flag: Shamrocks wreathed in gold - 'Scariff and civil and religious liberty' in gold letters. Mr O'Connell has been chaired to the Courthouse . . .
12 o'clock: There is not a drunken man in the streets, and, but for the shouting, everything is tranquil. About 600 men from Cratloe and Sixmilebridge marching eight and ten abreast have arrived carrying large laurel branches.

■ GLEANINGS

(a) There seems to have been only one polling station in all of County Clare. How does the *Freeman's Journal* report suggest this?

(b) Why, do you think, did the voters have to resort to green branches instead of banners and posters to show their allegiance?

(c) There were fifteen polling booths. How, do you think, were they organised?

(d) No women took part in the marches. Why, do you think, was that the case?

(e) Why were priests so openly involved in what was a political event?

(f) 'There is not a drunken man in the streets.' What does this sentence suggest to you?

■ FACT FILE

The election went on for five days, and O'Connell was elected MP for Clare by 2054 votes to 1075.

Because of O'Connell's success the government feared a rebellion if emancipation were not granted, and in 1829 the Emancipation Act granting some freedom to Catholics was passed.

O'Connell in triumphal procession through the streets

The repeal movement

Once the Emancipation Act was passed, O'Connell sought the removal of other laws against Catholics and succeeded in having some of them revoked by parliament. Then he began a campaign to have the Act of Union repealed. He held monster meetings in several parts of the country, and people turned up in their thousands to listen to him.

■ EXERCISE

Study this picture of one of the monster meetings. Imagine that you had been brought to the meeting by your father and could find a place only at the edge of the huge crowd. Write a diary entry (one paragraph) for that evening, describing the scene and telling of your experience.

The scene at one of O'Connell's monster meetings

■ FACT FILE

The meeting planned for Clontarf on Sunday, 8 October 1843, was banned by the government. O'Connell was committed to peaceful means of gaining his objectives and did not wish to confront soldiers and police sent to ensure the ban was obeyed. The committee called off the meeting, and that ended the agitation for repeal of the Union.

NOTICE.

WHEREAS, there has appeared, under the Signatures of "E. B. Sugden, C., Donoughmore, Eliot, F. Blackburne, E. Blakeney, Fred. Shaw, T. B. C. Smith," a paper being, or purporting to be, a PROCLAMATION, drawn up in very loose and inaccurate terms, and manifestly misrepresenting known facts; the objects of which appear to be, to prevent the PUBLIC MEETING, intended to be held TO-MORROW, the 8th instant, at CLONTARF, *to petition Parliament* for the REPEAL of the baleful and destructive measure of the LEGISLATIVE UNION.

AND WHEREAS, such Proclamation has not appeared until *late in the Afternoon of this Saturday, the 7th*, so that it is utterly impossible that the knowledge of its existence could be communicated in the usual Official Channels, or by the Post, in time to have its contents known to the Persons intending to meet at CLONTARF, for the purpose of Petitioning, as aforesaid, whereby ill-disposed Persons may have an opportunity, under cover of said Proclamation, to provoke Breaches of the Peace, or to commit Violence on Persons intending to proceed peaceably and legally to the said Meeting.

WE, therefore, the COMMITTEE of the LOYAL NATIONAL REPEAL ASSOCIATION, do most earnestly request and entreat, that all well-disposed persons will, IMMEDIATELY on receiving this intimation, repair to their own dwellings, and not place themselves in peril of any collision, or of receiving any ill-treatment whatsoever.

And We do further inform all such persons, that without yielding in any thing to the unfounded allegations in said alleged Proclamation, we deem it prudent and wise, and above all things humane, to DECLARE that said

Meeting is abandoned, and is not to be held.

Signed by Order,

DANIEL O'CONNELL,
Chairman of the Committee.

T. M. RAY, Secretary.

Saturday, 7th October, 1843.
3 o'Clock P. M.

RESOLVED—That the above Cautionary Notice be immediately transmitted by Express to the Very Reverend and Reverend Gentlemen who signed the Requisition for the CLONTARF MEETING, and to all adjacent Districts, SO AS TO PREVENT the influx of Persons coming to the intended Meeting.

GOD SAVE THE QUEEN.

The notice calling off the Clontarf meeting

◼ GLEANINGS

(a) Name the three things represented in the emblem at the top of the notice. Why, do you think, did the repeal movement agree to have a crown over the harp?

(b) What was the full name of the Repeal Association?

(c) Write the sentence which shows clearly that O'Connell and his committee were opposed to violence.

(d) Why, do you think, did the authorities delay issuing the proclamation until late in the afternoon of 7 October?

(e) Who were given the responsibility of displaying copies of the notice on the roads leading to the meeting venue?

(f) How was the notice sent to the Very Reverend and Reverend gentlemen?

■ FACT FILE

In 1845 the repeal movement split, as some of the members opposed O'Connell's view on the use of force. O'Connell died in 1847.

Looking south from Carlisle Bridge (now O'Connell Bridge), Dublin, in 1820

■ THINK AND WRITE

1 Who was the most important Irishman during the early part of the 19th century? _____

2 What special gifts did O'Connell possess?_____

_____

3 What did he witness while in France? _____

_____

4 What group backed him for the Clare elections? _____

_____

5 In what year were the Clare elections held? _____

_____

6 Who was O'Connell's opponent in the Clare election? _____

_____

7 Who was favourite to win the seat? _____

_____

8 Name another Irishman who won a very important election in County
Clare and was later president of Ireland. _____

_____

9 What was granted to Catholics in 1829? _____

_____

■ EXERCISE

Put words from the box in the spaces.

Clare	reforms	Association	Cahirciveen	1829
Act	violence	Revolution	Clontarf	
1847	followers	Union	Catholics	

Daniel O'Connell was born near _____, County Kerry.
From 1791 to 1793 he was in France, studying law. While in France
he saw the cruelty and bloodshed of the French _____, and
that gave him a hatred of _____.

O'Connell planned to use his knowledge of the law to win _____
for Catholics. In 1823 he founded the Catholic _____.
In 1828 he was elected to parliament for County _____. A bill
granting Catholic emancipation became law in _____. O'Connell
was then a hero of the Irish _____.

O'Connell decided that every effort should be made to repeal the
____ of _____. In October 1843 O'Connell had planned to hold
one of his biggest meetings at _____, County Dublin. The
government banned the meeting and O'Connell called it off,
much to the disappointment of his _____. O'Connell died in
_____.

THE GREAT FAMINE

■ FACT FILE

In 1841 a census showed that there were 8,175,000 people living in Ireland. The vast majority worked on the land. They lived on potatoes. One acre of ground grew enough potatoes to feed one family for most of the year.

In 1845 a total of 181,950 families lived on less than five acres, and a further 135,314 had less than one acre. In addition, many thousands of labourers had no land at all. A farmer paid his labourer by allowing him to use a patch of ground to grow potatoes to feed himself and his family.

The three-legged pot (skillet) in which the potatoes were boiled, and the basket (kish) in which they were strained and served.

■ EXERCISE

The home of a poor Irish family in the early years of the 19th century

Write a description of the scene in the above picture.

■ FACT FILE

Evidence before the Devon Commission

The Devon Commission was set up in 1843 to investigate poverty in Ireland. James Carey, a labourer with six children, gave the following evidence before the Commission in 1844.

Q:	How many meals a day have your family generally?
Carey:	Three.
Q:	Take breakfast – what do they have for breakfast?
Carey:	Potatoes and milk, unless we chance to buy a hundred of meal; then they have stirabout when the potatoes are bad.
Q:	Have they stirabout generally for breakfast?
Carey:	No, only now and then; at times we get potatoes for them and a sup of milk.

Q:	Do you always have milk?
Carey:	No, the cow is sometimes in calf.
Q:	What do you do then?
Carey:	Eat them dry.
Q:	Do the children ever get a herring or anything of that kind?
Carey:	Yes, when we have a penny to buy it, or a sup of gruel to take with the potatoes.
Q:	Do you ever get any butter?
Carey:	No.
Q:	How often a year do you get meat?
Carey:	We never get meat except a bit at Christmas, that would last for a week. We may chance to buy a half a pound of bacon on market day and dress a bit of greens with it and fry it.

■ GLEANINGS

(a) Why were the people so poor?
(b) Which did the Carey family prefer, meal or potatoes?
(c) What foods could a farmer produce on his land to add to those mentioned in Carey's account?
(d) Name some of the 'greens' which the people might have cooked with the bacon.

■ FACT FILE

The work house

The Poor Law of 1838 divided Ireland up into 130 districts, called unions. Each union was controlled by a board of guardians elected locally. The guardians raised money by imposing a tax on the union, and this 'poor rate' was used to build a workhouse to help the local poor.

A workhouse

A poor person needing help from the board of guardians had to go into the workhouse. The workhouses were made as uncomfortable as possible to ensure that only those who really needed help would go in.

The inmates of workhouses were given two meals a day: a breakfast of 7 ounces of oatmeal and a pint of buttermilk, and a dinner of 3 ½ pounds of potatoes and a pint of buttermilk. No alcohol, tobacco or tea was allowed. Meals were to be eaten in strict silence.

Men, women, and children were separated. People had to earn their keep, the men breaking stones, and the women spinning or knitting.

■ INTERVIEW

When some travellers asked one ragged man why he would not go into a workhouse, he replied:

'I'd rather share the fox's hole and lie down to die with the air of heaven above me as all my people did, than to be put alive into that poor man's gaol and be looked at by the quality like a show'.

■ GLEANINGS

(a) Why did the poor man call the workhouse a gaol?
(b) Who had the poor man in mind when he spoke of the 'quality'?
(c) What did the poor man mean by 'looked at by the quality like a show'?
(d) For what purpose were men given the job of breaking stones in the workhouse?
(e) Look at the plan of the workhouse, and tell how the layout enabled the authorities to keep men, women, and children apart.

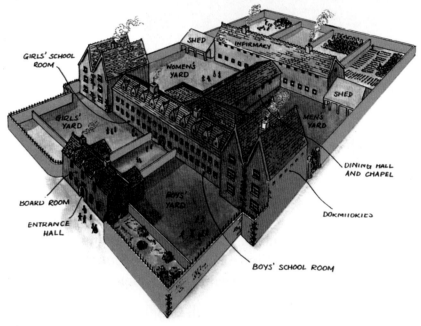

Plan of a workhouse

■ FACT FILE

The Great Hunger

Between 1845 and 1849 the potato crop in Ireland was attacked by a disease known as 'blight'. The crop was almost completely wiped out in three of those four years.

Because the potato was the staple food of the people, the effects were catastrophic: people were weakened by hunger, and famine fever spread. It was contagious and deadly. A million people died and another million emigrated.

Some attempts were made to help the starving people: the government set up public works, mainly laying and improving roads. Men on that work were paid 8 to 10 pence per day, enough to buy about a half stone of meal, and that was insufficient to feed a family. Some were helped by private charity.

In 1847 the government set up soup kitchens, and through the summer they were feeding over three million people a day.

Many people forgot their dislike of workhouses and those institutions were overcrowded.

Those who emigrated to America crossed the Atlantic in overcrowded ships in which fever raged. The poorest of the emigrants were forced to remain for the entire voyage in cramped quarters below deck. They had to live on badly cooked, poor food and were given very little water. The voyage could last up to three months and thousands died on the way.

The picture below shows the *Arthemisia* leaving Cork Harbour. The more wealthy passengers could afford a passage on deck. Write five sentences about the feelings of those left behind as the ship sailed away.

■ FROM A DIARY

Read these extracts from the diary of Humphrey O'Sullivan for July 1830. O'Sullivan was first a schoolmaster and later a linen draper who lived in Callan in County Kilkenny. These extracts are translated from the Irish, *Cín Lae Amhlaoibh*, by Tomás de Bhaldraithe.

July 26th

The paupers are picking potatoes out of the edges of the ridges. The 'black famine' is in their mouths. It would be hard for God to blame them, but, on the other hand it is a bad habit, for if the poor people start thieving and stealing, pillaging, plundering and taking by force will follow . . .

This month is now called Hungry July. Buímhís ('yellow month') is its proper name in Irish. It is a suitable name, for the fields are yellow, and also the faces of the paupers are greenish yellow from the black famine, as they live on green cabbage and poor scraps of that sort.

A fine warm day. I went swimming with my two sons Amhlaoibhín and Séamaisín. The water in the river was warm. There were many youths bathing there.

Ragged and starving

July 28th

Myself and two of the well-to-do people gave out a lot of yellow meal to the paupers of Callan, for twopence a pot. This is great relief to them.

July 30th

The food which I and my family eat is warm food, namely oatmeal porridge with milk in the morning, wheaten bread and milk at one o'clock. That is a cooling mid-day meal. Potatoes and meat, or butter in the coolness of the evening.

■ GLEANINGS

(a) The diary entries are for 1830. How do they show that if the potato crop were to fail, the poor people would be vulnerable?
(b) Were all the people in the country poor?
(c) The diarist condemned the poor people for stealing. Had they a choice?
(d) Write any sentence which, in your opinion, shows that the diarist had little compassion for the poor people.
(e) Compare his diet with that of James Carey (page 47-48).
(f) What language was spoken in Callan at the time?

■ EXERCISES

1 Compare conditions in Ireland in 1845 - 49 with those in places like Ethiopia, Somalia, and Rwanda today.
2 By what percentage was the population of Ireland reduced as a result of the famine?
3 Look at the picture of the poorest of the passengers confined below deck in one of the 'coffin' ships. Imagine you are one of them and write a page of the diary you kept during the voyage.

Below deck in a ship crossing the Atlantic at the time of the Great Famine

4   Read the following extract from Seamus Heaney's poem *For the Commander of the Eliza*. Imagine you are one of the people in the rowing boat. Tell your story.

For the Commander of the Eliza

Routine patrol off West Mayo; sighting
A rowboat heading unusually far
Beyond the creek, I tacked and hailed the crew
In Gaelic. Their stroke had clearly weakened
As they pulled to, from guilt or bashfulness
I was conjecturing when, O my sweet Christ,
We saw piled in the bottom of their craft
Six grown men with gaping mouths and eyes
Bursting the sockets like spring onions in drills.
Six wrecks of bone and pallid, tautened skin.
'Bia, bia,
Bia'. In whines and snarls their desperation
Rose and fell like a flock of starving gulls.

THE REVOLUTIONARY TRADITION

■ FACT FILE

The spirit of revolt

Although the 1798 rebellion was a failure, the spirit of revolt was not totally extinguished in Ireland. Like the corn that sprung from the Croppies' graves, it came to life again and again.

1803

In 1803 a poorly planned rebellion in Dublin, led by Robert Emmett, was easily defeated. Emmett was executed.

Robert Emmett's execution in Thomas Street, Dublin

1848

Among those in O'Connell's repeal movement who advocated force to achieve political aims was a group of young men who were given the nickname **Young Ireland**. When they split from O'Connell, they founded their own organisation, the **Irish Confederation**.

They staged a rebellion in 1848. The fighting took place mainly in the village of Ballingarry in County Tipperary. The insurrection ended shortly after the police arrived in Ballingarry. The rebels were weak, and, after a brief clash with police at the Widow McCormack's house, their leader, William Smith O'Brien, ordered them to disperse.

Prominent among those involved were **James Stephens** and **John O'Mahony**.

The battle at the Widow McCormack's house in Ballingarry

The Fenians: 1867

The spirit of revolt was carried to America in the emigrant ships, and it was from America that the drive for the 1867 rebellion came.

After 1848 James Stephens fled to Paris, and he met John O'Mahony there. They decided that it was time to take up arms again. O'Mahony went to America, and Stephens returned to Ireland.

In 1858 Stephens founded the **Irish Republican Brotherhood** (IRB), and at about the same time O'Mahony founded a similar society in America, the **Fenian Brotherhood of America**. Both organisations came to be known as the **Fenians**.

Policemen searching for arms

The IRB was a secret, oath-bound society, but almost from the beginning it was riddled with government spies. Many of the Fenians were arrested, including James Stephens, but he escaped from prison and went to America. Later he was replaced as leader by Colonel James Kelly.

A few skirmishes took place, including a small rising in Cahirciveen in Kerry. The main rising was planned for 6 March 1867. It was a night of heavy snow, yet several thousand Fenians rose up in Dublin, Cork, Limerick, Tipperary, and other places. They were ill-prepared, unarmed, and were easily defeated.

THINK AND WRITE

1 Where did the drive for the 1867 rising come from? _____

_____

2 Who founded the IRB? _____

3 What society was founded in America by John O'Mahony? _____

_____

4 How did the government find out the names of those in the IRB? _____

_____

5 Who replaced James Stephens as leader? _____

A BALLAD

Read the following two verses from *The Bold Fenian Men*, written
by Michael Scanlan (1836 - 1900).

We've men from the Nore, from the Suir and the Shannon.
Let tyrants come forth, we'll bring force against force.
Our pen is the sword and our voice is the cannon,
Rifle for rifle and horse against horse.
We've made the false Saxon yield many a red battlefield.
God on our side we will triumph again.
Oh pay them back woe for woe, give them back blow for blow.
Out and make way for the Bold Fenian Men.

Side by side for our cause have our forefathers battled
Where our hills never echoed the tread of a slave.
On many green hills where the leaden hail rattled,
Through the red gap of glory they marched to their grave.
And those who inherit their name and their spirit
Will march 'neath the banners of Liberty then.
And all who love Saxon law, native or Sassenach,
Out and make way for the Bold Fenian Men.

GLEANINGS

(a) Why, in your opinion, did Michael Scanlan write this ballad?

(b) Pick out two lines which seem boastful to you and say whether you think the boasts were justified.

(c) Finish this sentence: The fifth and sixth lines of the second verse illustrate the title of this unit because they are about

_____

(d) What, do you think, did the writer mean by 'our pen is the sword, and our voice is the cannon'?

(e) Who, do you think, were the natives who loved Saxon law?

(f) What is meant by each of the following phrases:
  • our hills never echoed the tread of a slave
  • where the leaden hail rattled
  • the red gap of glory?

Soldiers searching for Fenians

HOME RULE AND PARNELL

■ FACT FILE

Robert Emmett in 1803, the Young Irelanders in 1848 and the Fenians in 1867 failed to obtain some form of home rule for Ireland by the use of force. Nationalists turned once again to politics to try to win for Ireland its own parliament to run its own affairs.

Isaac Butt was a lawyer and an MP who supported Prime Minister Gladstone. He called a meeting in Dublin in 1870 of people interested in the welfare of Ireland, and the **Home Rule Association** was founded. The Home Rule Association pressed for an Irish parliament within the United Kingdom of Great Britain and Ireland whereas the Fenians wanted complete independence from Britain. The Home Rule Party contested an election in 1874 and won 59 seats, but they found it hard to get the parliament to take a serious interest in Irish affairs.

A Wicklow man, **Charles Stewart Parnell,** was elected a Home Rule MP for County Meath in 1875 at the age of 29. He was a landlord and a Protestant nationalist.

In 1880 he became leader of the Home Rule Party. He also became the first president of the Land League (see Unit 10). He joined together with **Michael Davitt**, the founder of the Land League, and with **John Devoy**, the leader of the Fenians, against the British government.

Isaac Butt   *Charles S. Parnell*   *Michael Davitt*   *John Devoy*

Parnell became a national hero, getting massive support from farmers all over Ireland.

He was a powerful, strong and forceful leader and became known as 'The Chief'. He built up a strong party and finally persuaded Gladstone to agree to Home Rule for Ireland.

But the unionists feared that they would not be treated fairly in a parliament with a majority of Southern Catholics. The Conservative Party backed the Ulster unionists, and the Home Rule Bill of 1886 was defeated.

■ LOOKING AT THE PICTURE

In the picture below you can see an anti-Home Rule riot in Belfast.

Compare the scene in this picture with some happenings in recent times. What is different now?

■ FROM AN EYEWITNESS

The following passage is taken from *The Farm by Lough Gur* by Mary Carbery. Bessie, one of three sisters, wished to meet Parnell, and one day their parish priest calls to the house.

'More Irish than the Irish themselves, that's what the man is, God bless him – for all his foreign blood which is none of his fault, and his heresy which please God we'll cure him of,' said Father Burke.

Bessie was trembling and pale from the shock she had had. 'Protestant,' she gasped, 'descended from Sassenach invaders?'

'Come here, my young rebel,' Father Burke ordered. 'I've looked in here to invite your mother and father, and perhaps one or two of you little girls to a meeting in Limerick where you'll see and hear – Mr Parnell!'

My head whirled and my heart thumped. Here was the chance of a lifetime to see a great man, Ireland's great man!

Father and Mother, Bessie and I went in the morning. We saw Mr Parnell quite closely. He looked tired, his face was pale, his dark eyes glowed in their deep sockets. When our parents were introduced by Father Burke, he shook hands and spoke to them in his English voice and then nodded to us, 'How do, how do,' he said, looking equally at Bessie and me and without a smile for either of us. We had secretly agreed to genuflect as we do in chapel, but there was not time before he turned away. When we told Mother of our thwarted intention, she said she was glad we hadn't made ourselves noticeable. She would have been ashamed.

Strange as it may be, that meeting with her hero seemed to make Bessie more sensible. She attended to her lessons and we heard less rebel talk. As for me I was glad to have seen Mr Parnell and that was that.

■ GLEANINGS

(a) Who was the rebel in the family?
(b) Why, do you think, did Parnell pay little attention to the girls?
(c) Which did the family support, the Fenian way or the Home Rule Party way of seeking independence? Give a reason for your answer.
(d) Why, do you think, did Parnell look tired?
(e) Why, do you think, did Bessie give up her rebel talk?

(f) The family lived near Lough Gur in the south-east of County Limerick and about twenty miles from Limerick City. How did they travel to the city to meet Parnell?

(g) What did Father Burke mean when he said they would cure him of his heresy?

(h) Why did the Catholic Irish people trust a man who was a 'Sassenach' and a Protestant?

■ FACT FILE

In 1890 it was announced that Parnell was to marry Katherine O'Shea, a woman who had recently been divorced. This upset many of his Catholic followers, and some of them abandoned him.

The country split into two camps, those for and those against Parnell. This weakened the Home Rule Party.

The Home Rule Party, too, was split, and some of the members asked Parnell to resign as leader. This Parnell refused to do. He returned to Ireland and went through the country making speeches asking for support. But many, including the Catholic bishops, were opposed to him. His followers were beaten in three by-elections.

In 1891 Parnell caught pneumonia and died at 45 years of age, fourteen weeks after his wedding day. He is buried in Glasnevin cemetery in Dublin.

■ EXERCISE

This picture shows Parnell speaking to the people during one of the by-elections. Describe the attitude of the crowd to Parnell's speech.

■ THINK AND WRITE

1 Who formed the Home Rule Party? _____

_____

2 For what county was Parnell elected an MP? _____

_____

3 Parnell himself was a landlord in County _____

4 What position did Parnell hold in the Land League? _____

_____

5 What year did Parnell become leader of the Home Rule Party? _____

_____

6 Parnell was often referred to as (a) _____

(b) _____

7 What prime minister did Parnell persuade to grant Home Rule to Ireland? _____

_____

8 Who prevented Home Rule being given to Ireland? _____

_____

9 What caused the majority of Irish people to turn against Parnell? _____

_____

10 What was the cause of Parnell's death in 1891? _____

_____

THE LAND LEAGUE

■ FACT FILE

After the famine

The famine's greatest toll was among those who worked the land. Many of them died or emigrated, and that gave landlords the opportunity to let the land to those who could pay the rent. Some of the landlords decided to make their estates into vast ranches of grassland for cattle and sheep.

The Land Act of 1870

The British prime minister, William Gladstone, wanted to give Irish tenants a right to the land they were farming. In 1870 he introduced a Land Act which stated that as long as the tenant farmers paid their rent, they could not be evicted from the land. However, a landlord was allowed to retain his right to increase the rent.

In the late 1870s, crops failed and thousands of tenants could not pay their rents. Many were threatened with eviction, but they were not willing to give up the land without a fight.

Prime Minister Gladstone

The Land League

To organise tenants in a movement to press for a fair deal from landlords, Michael Davitt founded a society, which he called the **Land League**, in Co. Mayo in 1879. Parnell became the first president of the Land League. The aim of the new society was to defend the rights of tenants and to break the power of the landlords. Some money was sent from the Fenians in America to help the Land League.

The league's three aims were:

1 Fair rent
2 Fixity of tenure
3 Free sale of the tenant's holding.

These became known as the **'Three F's'**.

■ PEN PORTRAIT

Michael Davitt

Michael Davitt was born in 1846 in Straide in County Mayo. His father was a small farmer. When Michael was five years old, the family were evicted from their farm because they could not pay the rent.

The Davitts moved to England, where Michael was sent to work in a cotton mill in Lancashire. When he was eleven years old, he was victim of an accident in the mill. His right arm was caught in a machine and it had to be amputated.

In 1865 he joined the Fenians and in 1870 was arrested for gun-running and sentenced to fifteen years in prison. He was released after seven years and returned to Ireland. He founded the National Land League in 1879. He died in 1906.

■ THINK AND WRITE

1 Why were many farmers unable to pay their rent in the late 1870s? _____

2 What did Michael Davitt do to help? _____
_____

3 What were the aims of the Land League? _____
_____

4 Who was British prime minister in 1870? _____

5 When was the Land League established? _____

■ EXERCISES

1 What do you think happened when a tenant was evicted?
    Draw a picture of an eviction scene.
2 Write a letter to Michael Davitt to tell him that the rent on
    your farm has been increased and that you will not be able to pay it.

■ FACT FILE

The land war

Branches of the Land League were set up in many parts of the country. If rents were made too high by the landlord, the tenants were urged not to pay. However, landlords had the law on their side and many tenants were evicted by force. This struggle became known as the 'land war'.

Boycott

Captain Charles Boycott lived in County Mayo near Lough Mask. He was a landlord's agent and his job was to set rents and collect the money from tenant farmers. He raised the rents to an unfair level and refused to lower them.

A load of turf for a landlord being dumped by Land Leaguers

In autumn 1880, members of the Land League decided to have nothing whatsoever to do with Captain Boycott. None of his workers, servants or neighbours would do anything for him. Nobody would sell him anything or even speak to him. This plan by the Land League gave the word 'boycott' to the English language.

◼ EXERCISES

1 Choose the correct answer. Write out the full sentence.

    A   Michael Davitt was born in

        (a) County Monaghan
        (b) County Mayo
        (c) County Meath.

    B   When the Davitts were evicted, they went to

        (a) America
        (b) England
        (c) Dublin.

    C The three F's of the Land League were

        (a) Fair rent, Fixity of tenure, Freedom to sell
        (b) Freedom, Fairness, Fighting
        (c) Famine, Food, Fortitude.

    D Michael Davitt lost his right arm in

        (a) a road accident
        (b) an accident in a cotton mill
        (c) an accident in a saw mill.

    E   An eviction means

        (a) tenants are put out of their house
        (b) the landlord increases the rent
        (c) people are going to live in another country.

2 Design and colour a poster for a Land League meeting as if it were about to take place in your county.

An eviction scene

3 (a) What is happening in this picture?
   (b) Who, do you think, is the man in the tall hat? Give a
        reason for your answer.
   (c) What is happening to the tenants' furniture?
   (d) Why are the police there?
   (e) Where, do you think, will the people who live in this house go?

■ FACT FILE

The Land Acts

In 1881 a law was passed by Prime Minister Gladstone, stating that
fair rents would in future be fixed by a court. He was anxious to
end the unrest about the land and to bring an end to the land war.

However, the Land League demanded that people be allowed to buy
out their land and that they should be given help from the government
to do this.

A Land League demonstration

The Land League urged their followers to withhold rent. Because of this the leaders of the Land League were imprisoned in Kilmainham Jail in Dublin for seven months. But the movement continued to press for change, and other laws were passed to give help to people who wished to buy out their land.

In 1903 the last of the Land Acts was passed which finally broke the power of the landlords.

■ THINK AND WRITE

1 Look up the meaning of the word 'boycott' in your dictionary and write a definition in your own words. _____

_____

2 Explain how the word 'boycott' came into the English language. _____

_____

3 Where was Parnell born? _____

_____

4 What county did he represent in parliament?_____

_____

5 Why did many of his followers later abandon him? _____

_____

6 Where is Parnell buried? _____

_____

7 What office did Parnell hold in the Land League?_____

_____

8 Was the Home Rule Bill of 1886 passed by parliament? _____

_____

9 Who was prime minister of Britain at the time of the land war? _____

_____

10 When was the last of the Land Acts passed? _____

_____

■ EXERCISES

1 Imagine you are Captain Boycott. Write an account in your
  diary for three days telling how nobody in the area will do
  anything for you.
2 Can you think of a time when 'boycotting' could be used
  effectively today?

THE GAELIC REVIVAL

■ FACT FILE

Towards the end of the 1800s the work of Davitt and Parnell helped to raise the spirits of the Irish people. Ordinary Irish men and women began to take a new pride in Ireland and in things that are native to this country. New movements were set up to promote the Irish language, Irish literature, and Irish games and customs.

Irish games

In 1884, **Michael Cusack**, **Archbishop Croke**, and friends founded the **Gaelic Athletic Association** (GAA). The meeting to set up the organisation was held in Thurles, County Tipperary, and its first patron was Archbishop Croke. The association was founded to organise hurling, football, handball and athletics. Rules were drawn up, and games and competitions were organised. The first All Ireland Final was played in 1887.

■ EXERCISE

This picture shows the new Cusack stand in Croke Park on All-Ireland Hurling Final day.

How did the stand and the stadium get their names? Write the answer.

FACT FILE

The Irish language

Ever since the famine the use of the Irish language had been declining and by the end of the 1800s it was spoken only in more remote areas along the west coast. Even in the national schools, which had been established in 1831, Irish was not taught or spoken.

In 1893, **Conradh na Gaeilge** (The Gaelic League) was set up to encourage people to speak Irish again, to sing Irish songs and dance Irish dances, and to write in the Irish language.

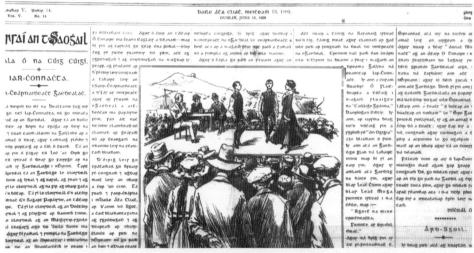

Part of front page of 'An Claidheamh Soluis'

Conradh na Gaeilge had its own newspaper called *An Claidheamh Soluis*. The Conradh also organised classes to teach the Irish language and Irish music.

Dr. Douglas Hyde became the first president of Conradh na Gaeilge. **Eoin McNeill** was a founder member.

Douglas Hyde

Eoin McNeill

THINK AND WRITE

1 In what town was the first GAA meeting held? _____

2 From whom does Croke Park get its name? _____

3 What games does the GAA organise? _____

4 Why was Conradh na Gaeilge established? _____

5 Who became first president of Conradh na Gaeilge? _____

6 What newspaper was published by Conradh na Gaeilge? _____

7 When were national schools first established in Ireland? _____

8 What do the letters GAA stand for? _____

■ EXERCISES

1 Draw a poster telling people about the new organisation called the Gaelic Athletic Association.
2 Draw and colour flags to represent the current All Ireland Football and Hurling Champions.
3 *An Claidheamh Soluis* means 'the sword of light'. Draw a suitable logo for the paper.

■ FACT FILE

Anglo-Irish literature

At this time great Irish writers were writing in English about Irish topics. **George Bernard Shaw** was one of them. The world-famous Irish poet, **W. B. Yeats**, wrote poems and plays about ancient Irish heroes, and Irish people were becoming proud of being Irish.

In 1904 **Lady Gregory** and W. B. Yeats established the **Abbey Theatre** in Dublin. This theatre soon became famous all over the world.

George Bernard Shaw   *W. B. Yeats*   *Lady Gregory*

New political movements

In 1905, **Arthur Griffith** established a new political organisation called **Sinn Féin** which means 'ourselves'. Its aim was to establish an Irish parliament to govern Ireland and to encourage people to buy goods made in this country in order to help Irish workers.

James Larkin and **James Connnolly** worked to help Irish workers. They were the founders of the labour movement. They organised Irish workers into a trade union.

Arthur Griffith

James Larkin

James Connolly

■ THINK AND WRITE

1 In what year was the Abbey Theatre in Dublin set up? _____

2 What is G.B. Shaw's full name? _____

3 What do the words 'Sinn Féin' mean? _____

4 What were the aims of Sinn Féin? _____
   _____

5 Name two leaders of the labour movement in Ireland. _____
   _____

■ EXERCISES

1 How would you encourage people to take pride in being Irish today?

2 Look up the newspaper and find the name of the play that is currently playing in the Abbey Theatre in Dublin.

3 Write an advertisement, including a picture, for a play in the Abbey Theatre.

■ TEST YOURSELF QUIZ 2

1 Who won the Clare election in 1828?
2 What was Daniel O'Connell's profession?
3 Why, do you think, was Daniel O'Connell opposed to violence?
4 When did Daniel O'Connell die?
5 What was the most common food eaten by the people at the beginning of the famine?
6 Which was the worst of the famine years?
7 How did the Great Famine affect the population of Ireland?
8 Where did poor people have to go to get food and accommodation?
9 What were 'coffin ships'?
10 What was the name of the disease that struck the potato crop at the time of the Great Famine?
11 What were the 'Three F's'?
12 Who founded the Land League?
13 How did the word 'boycott' enter the English language?
14 What movement was founded by James Stephens?
15 Who were involved in the rebellions of (a) 1803 (b) 1848 (c) 1867?
16 What party was founded by Isaac Butt in 1874?
17 Who became Home Rule MP for County Meath in 1875?
18 Who was the divorced woman married by Charles Stewart Parnell?
19 In what year did Parnell die?
20 Why did Michael Davitt dislike landlords?
21 Who founded the GAA?
22 Who founded Conradh na Gaeilge?
23 What was 'An Claidheamh Soluis'?
24 What was meant by 'Home Rule'?
25 Name two men who founded the labour movement in Ireland.

THE MOVE TO INDEPENDENCE

■ FACT FILE

Home Rule movement revived

The Home Rule Party, which had split at the time of Parnell's involvement in the O'Shea divorce affair, became united again under the leadership of **John Redmond** in 1910.

The British prime minister, Asquith, needed the support of the Home Rule Party in parliament, so he introduced a Home Rule Bill in 1912.

Opposition to Home Rule

The opposition to Home Rule among the Ulster unionists was intense. Their leaders were **Edward Carson** and **James Craig**. They formed the **Ulster Volunteer Force** (UVF) to resist any move to Home Rule.

The UVF intended to use arms if necessary, and a large cargo of guns and ammunition was landed at Larne in April 1914. No move was made by the authorities to prevent them from obtaining the guns. They began to drill and march to prepare for battle.

John Redmond

James Craig

Edward Carson

Carson inspects Ulster Volunteers

The Irish Volunteers

In Southern Ireland the Irish Volunteers were formed in 1913 to advance the cause of Home Rule. **Eoin McNeill** called for their formation in an article in *An Claidheamh Soluis*, and he became chief of staff. However, many important positions in the organisation were held by members of the IRB, a secret society.

Guns for the Irish Volunteers were landed in 1914 from a private yacht, the *Asgard*. The guns were removed to safety in spite of attempts by the army and police to prevent it. Later that day a jeering crowd in Bachelor's Walk in Dublin was fired on by British soldiers and three people were killed.

Irish Volunteers with some of the guns landed from the Asgard

■ THINK AND WRITE

1 Why did Asquith want to give Ireland Home Rule? _____

_____

2 Why were the Ulster unionists opposed to Home Rule? _____

_____

_____

3 What similarities were there between the UVF and the Irish Volunteers?

_____

4 How did the attitudes of police and army to the UVF differ from their
attitude to the Irish Volunteers? _____

_____

5 How was this difference in attitude shown? _____

_____

6 Why, do you think, did police and army not intervene in the Larne
gun-running? _____

_____

■ FACT FILE

Postponing Home Rule

With both volunteer forces armed, a civil war seemed likely.

A war in Europe, with Britain involved, seemed certain at that
time, so Asquith wanted to settle the Home Rule question without
delay. The Home Rule Bill was finally passed in 1914, but there
were two very important provisions in it:

1 The bill would not come into effect until after the war in
    Europe.
2 Some special arrangements would have to be made for the
    Ulster unionists.

The First World War

There was a split in the Irish Volunteers when the war in Europe broke out between Britain and France on one side and Germany on the other. Redmond urged the Volunteers to help Britain in the war because of the promise of Home Rule to follow. Some Volunteers fought on the British side, but a minority, led by the IRB, refused to do so. The IRB aimed for a completely independent republic and would not be satisfied with a Home Rule parliament within the British system.

■ EXERCISE

If you had lived in 1914, which would you have favoured, Home Rule or complete independence from Britain? Give a reason for your answer.

■ FACT FILE

The Irish Citizen Army

Eoin McNeill, the chief of staff of the Irish Volunteers, was not a member of the IRB and was not involved in an IRB plan to use the Volunteers in a rebellion.

Labour unrest in 1913 led to a lock-out of workers. James Larkin, the leader of the ITGWU (Irish Transport and General Workers' Union) held a number of public meetings which were broken up by the police. Larkin founded the **Irish Citizen Army** to protect the people attending the meetings.

■ EXERCISE

The Irish Citizen Army at Liberty Hall in Dublin

Write what you think the notice above the door means.

■ FACT FILE

When the lock-out ended, James Connolly became the leader of the Irish Citizen Army. Connolly was born in Edinburgh in Scotland, but came to Ireland and was a trade union organiser in Belfast. He began to train the Irish Citizen Army for a rebellion.

When the IRB heard that Connolly planned a rising, they decided to join with him.

REASONS WHY

YOU SHOULD JOIN

The Irish Citizen Army.

BECAUSE It pledges its members to work for, organise for, drill for and fight for **an Independent Ireland.**

BECAUSE It places its reliance upon the only class that never betrayed Ireland—the Irish Working Class.

BECAUSE Having a definite aim to work for there is no fear of it being paralysed in the moment of action by divisions in its Executive Body.

BECAUSE It teaches that "the sole right of ownership of Ireland is vested in the people of Ireland, and that that full right of ownership may, and ought to be, enforced by any and all means that God hath put within the power of man."

BECAUSE It works in harmony with the Labour and true National Movements and thus embraces all that makes for Social Welfare and National Dignity.

Companies Wanted in Every District.

RECRUITS WANTED EVERY HOUR.

Apply for further information, Secretary, Citizen Army, Liberty Hall, Dublin.

Irish Paper.]   *City Printing Works, 13 Stafford Street, Dublin.*

(a) To whom would you write if you wished to join the Irish Citizen Army?
(b) Which of the reasons given for joining the Citizen Army would you think the most important? Give a reason for your choice.
(c) Why, do you think, did they want people to know that the notice was printed on Irish paper?
(d) What were the aims of the Irish Citizen Army?
(e) How did they hope to achieve their aims?
(f) What was the name of the headquarters of the Irish Citizen Army?
(g) Why, do you think, did the notice make the point that the Citizen Army's executive was 'in no fear of it being paralysed' by divisions?

THE EASTER RISING: 1916

■ FACT FILE

Planning the rising

The IRB appointed a committee of five men to plan a rebellion. Their plans were kept secret, and only the five knew what was afoot until shortly before the rising took place. Their greatest problem was to involve the Irish Volunteers in the rising because their chief of staff, Eoin McNeill, was opposed to it unless there was a realistic chance of success.

The First World War, which occupied Britain in Europe from 1914 to 1918, gave the IRB the opportunity to stage their rebellion.

The Irish Volunteers were accustomed to taking part in manoeuvres on public holidays. They did not realise that the IRB was planning to use them in a rebellion when they prepared for an outing on Easter Sunday 1916.

Roger Casement went to Germany to obtain guns for a rebellion in Ireland. An attempt to land the guns on Banna Strand near Tralee in County Kerry failed when the British captured the gun-running German ship, the *Aud*, and arrested Casement.

When McNeill learned that a rising had been planned and that an attempt to land German guns in Kerry had failed, he put an advertisement in the Sunday Independent calling off the Volunteer manoeuvres planned for the Easter weekend.

However, the IRB Military Council decided to go ahead with the rising on Easter Monday. By this time the IRB Military Council had seven members. Those members were later to sign the proclamation of the provisional government of the Irish Republic at the beginning of the rebellion.

■ GLEANINGS

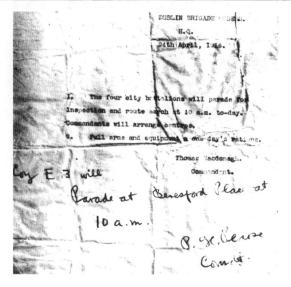

McNeill's order cancelling the training exercises for the Easter weekend

MacDonagh's and Pearse's orders to their battalions

(a) Note the dates of the two orders. If you were a Volunteer, which order would you obey?
(b) Why did McNeill say that Volunteers had been deceived?
(c) Did MacDonagh expect the fighting to last a long time? Give a reason for your answer.
(d) How many battalions of the Volunteers were in Dublin?
(e) Which was bigger, a brigade or a battalion?

■ FACT FILE

Easter 1916

About 1600 Volunteers, including James Connolly's Citizen Army, marched through the city of Dublin and occupied some of the important buildings. They occupied the GPO which was to be their headquarters, the Four Courts, St. Stephen's Green and other places. The garrison at Boland's Mills was under the command of Éamon de Valera.

The people on O'Connell Street were amazed to see Patrick Pearse reading a proclamation from the steps of the GPO. The proclamation was signed by the IRB leaders.

Thomas MacDonagh

Eamonn Ceannt

Joseph Plunkett

POBLACHT NA H EIREANN.

THE PROVISIONAL GOVERNMENT
OF THE
IRISH REPUBLIC
TO THE PEOPLE OF IRELAND.

IRISHMEN AND IRISHWOMEN : In the name of God and of the dead generations from which she receives her old tradition of nationhood, Ireland, through us, summons her children to her flag and strikes for her freedom.

Having organised and trained her manhood through her secret revolutionary organisation, the Irish Republican Brotherhood, and through her open military organisations, the Irish Volunteers and the Irish Citizen Army, having patiently perfected her discipline, having resolutely waited for the right moment to reveal itself, she now seizes that moment, and, supported by her exiled children in America and by gallant allies in Europe, but relying in the first on her own strength, she strikes in full confidence of victory.

We declare the right of the people of Ireland to the ownership of Ireland, and to the unfettered control of Irish destinies, to be sovereign and indefeasible. The long usurpation of that right by a foreign people and government has not extinguished the right, nor can it ever be extinguished except by the destruction of the Irish people. In every generation the Irish people have asserted their right to national freedom and sovereignty; six times during the past three hundred years they have asserted it in arms. Standing on that fundamental right and again asserting it in arms in the face of the world, we hereby proclaim the Irish Republic as a Sovereign Independent State, and we pledge our lives and the lives of our comrades-in-arms to the cause of its freedom, of its welfare, and of its exaltation among the nations.

The Irish Republic is entitled to, and hereby claims, the allegiance of every Irishman and Irishwoman. The Republic guarantees religious and civil liberty, equal rights and equal opportunities to all its citizens, and declares its resolve to pursue the happiness and prosperity of the whole nation and of all its parts, cherishing all the children of the nation equally, and oblivious of the differences carefully fostered by an alien government, which have divided a minority from the majority in the past.

Until our arms have brought the opportune moment for the establishment of a permanent National Government, representative of the whole people of Ireland and elected by the suffrages of all her men and women, the Provisional Government, hereby constituted, will administer the civil and military affairs of the Republic in trust for the people.

We place the cause of the Irish Republic under the protection of the Most High God, Whose blessing we invoke upon our arms, and we pray that no one who serves that cause will dishonour it by cowardice, inhumanity, or rapine. In this supreme hour the Irish nation must, by its valour and discipline and by the readiness of its children to sacrifice themselves for the common good, prove itself worthy of the august destiny to which it is called.

Signed on Behalf of the Provisional Government,

THOMAS J. CLARKE.
SEAN Mac DIARMADA,   THOMAS MacDONAGH,
P. H. PEARSE,   EAMONN CEANNT,
JAMES CONNOLLY.   JOSEPH PLUNKETT.

Seán MacDiarmada

P.H. Pearse

James Connolly

Thomas J. Clarke

■ THINK AND WRITE

1 According to the proclamation, three Irish organisations played a major part in the rising. Name them. _____

_____

2 Name the leaders of the provisional government. _____

_____

_____

3 Under whose protection did the leaders place their cause? _____

_____

4 What Irish company uses the GPO now? _____

_____

5 In what street is the GPO in Dublin? _____

_____

6 To whom was the proclamation addressed? _____

_____

7 What was guaranteed to Irish citizens? _____

_____

8 What were all the children in the nation promised?   (a) _____
   (b) _____   (c) _____

9 Who had a right to ownership of Ireland according to the proclamation? _____

_____

10 Find the meanings of the following words in your dictionary:
   indefeasible _____

   usurpation _____

   suffrages _____

   rapine _____

■ PEN PORTRAIT

Patrick H. Pearse: 1879 - 1916

- Born in Dublin
- Trained as barrister
- Great interest in the Irish language
- Joined Volunteers and IRB
- Poet
- Opened a school in Rathfarnham, Dublin
- Inspired students with love of Ireland
- In a speech at the grave of the Fenian O'Donovan Rossa, he said, *'Ireland unfree shall never be at peace'*.

■ THINK AND WRITE

1 What age was Patrick Pearse when he was executed? _____

_____

2 What two military organisations did he join? _____

_____

3 Where did he open his school, St Enda's? _____

_____

4 Explain what you think he meant when he said, *'Ireland unfree shall never be at peace'*. _____

_____

■ FACT FILE

The rising began on Easter Monday, 24 April 1916, and lasted until the following Saturday. The British brought a gunboat up the Liffey and shelled the GPO. When the rebels surrendered, over five hundred people had been killed, and the centre of the city was in ruins.

Dublin city centre after the rising

The people of Dublin were angry at what had happened to their city and had little sympathy with the rebels. As the rebel leaders were being led to prison they were jeered on the way.

However, the mood changed when the British decided to execute fifteen of the leaders. Among those who were executed were the seven who signed the proclamation. Soon the people who took part in the 1916 rising became heroes.

■ THINK AND WRITE

1 When did the First World War begin? _____
_____

2 Why did so many Irishmen join the British army? _____
_____

3 Name one group of Irish people who did not support the British. _____
_____

4 Name the leader of the Irish Volunteers. _____
_____

5 Who was in charge in the Irish Citizen Army? _____
_____

6 On what date did the Easter Rising begin? _____
_____

7 How long did the rising last? _____
_____

8 How many were killed during the rising? _____
_____

9 Why were the rebels jeered as they were led to prison? _____
_____

10 Why did the people soon change their minds about the rebels? _____
_____

11 'Volunteers completely deceived. All orders for tomorrow Sunday entirely
cancelled'. Who wrote this? _____
_____

A NEW STATE IS BORN

■ FACT FILE

Although Sinn Féin did not take part in the 1916 rebellion, they were given much of the credit for it as they were the only political party seeking complete independence from Britain. The party became popular and many new members joined.

In 1917 Sinn Féin won four by-elections, including a win by Éamon de Valera in Clare. The IRB and the Irish Volunteers decided to work together with Sinn Féin towards obtaining complete independence from Britain.

At the Sinn Féin Árd Fheis in 1917 Arthur Griffith agreed to the election of Éamon de Valera as president of Sinn Féin.

The war in Europe ended in 1918, and a general election was held. Sinn Féin won 73 seats, the Home Rule Party 6. The new Sinn Féin members of parliament refused to take their seats to assert their aim of complete independence from Britain.

The first Dáil: 1919

The new Sinn Féin members of parliament decided to set up their own parliament. The first Dáil met in the Mansion House in Dublin on 21 January 1919. Only 27 of the elected members attended. Of those who were absent, 34 were in prison.

They declared Ireland to be independent and established the manner in which Dáil members were to be elected. They sent a message to the free nations of the world asking for recognition for the new republic. They set up their own courts to replace the English courts.

The first meeting of Dáil Éireann

■ THINK AND WRITE

1 Why were the Irish leaders jeered by the people after the 1916 rebellion?

_____

2 Why did people soon change their minds about the rising? _____

_____

3 Which party won most of the Irish seats in the 1918 election? _____

_____

4 Who was elected president of Sinn Féin? _____

_____

5 When did the first Dáil meet? _____

6 Where did the first Dáil meet? _____

7 What organisation declared Ireland a republic? _____

_____

8 What message did the new Dáil send to the nations of the world? _____

_____

■ FACT FILE

Guerrilla warfare: 1919 - 1921

After the 1916 rising the Irish Volunteers changed their name to the **Irish Republican Army** (IRA). They began to ambush the police (RIC) and the British army. They attacked police barracks to capture guns.

The Black and Tans

A new force recruited in Britain from the soldiers who served in the European war were given the nickname 'Black and Tans' because of the uniforms they wore, which were a mixture of RIC black and army khaki. A guerrilla war followed between British forces and the IRA. It was fought with great savagery at times.

■ EXERCISE

British patrols in Dublin

Why, do you think, was the patrol car covered in wire mesh?
Write your answer.

■ FACT FILE

Both sides carried out assassinations during this period. One of those murdered by the British forces was Tomás Mac Curtain, the Lord Mayor of Cork. His successor, Terence MacSwiney, died on hunger strike in Brixton Prison in London.

Michael Collins was prominent in the IRA. He was Director of Intelligence, and in the Dáil he was Minister of Defence.

Government of Ireland Act

The British parliament passed the Government of Ireland Act in 1920. This act gave the six counties of Northern Ireland Home Rule, and a parliament was set up there which lasted until it was suspended in 1972.

A truce

In July 1921 a truce was declared. In October talks about a treaty began in London. The Irish side included Arthur Griffith and Michael Collins, and the British side was led by Prime Minister **Lloyd George** and included Winston Churchill.

Lloyd George

The treaty

In the treaty, it was agreed that

1   Northern Ireland would continue to have a Home Rule parliament unless it wished to join the new state to be set up in the south.

2   the twenty-six counties of Southern Ireland were to form a new state called the **Irish Free State**.

3   the king would be represented by a governor general, and the members of the Irish Free State parliament would have to take an oath of allegiance to the king.

Debating the treaty

The Dáil was divided on the treaty.

Arguments for the treaty:

1 We have our own government, army, police force, and flag.
2 The king is in London and cannot now interfere in our affairs.
3 It was not possible to get a better deal.

Arguments against the treaty:

1 If we take an oath to the king, we cannot be called a real republic.
2 The British can still interfere in our affairs.
3 You were tricked by the prime minister. You have to return and get more for your country.

When the Dáil voted in January 1922, those in favour of accepting the treaty won by 64 votes to 57.

De Valera and his supporters, who were opposed to the treaty, abandoned the Dáil and decided to boycott it.

Civil war

A civil war which lasted until the summer of 1923 followed. A cease-fire was declared and those against the treaty surrendered. By then the new Irish state had been established according to the terms of the treaty.

Arthur Griffith died of overwork on 12 August 1922. Ten days later Michael Collins was killed in an ambush at Béal na mBláth in West Cork.

The funeral of Arthur Griffith

■ THINK AND WRITE

1 What did the first Dáil do at its first meeting? _____
_____

2 Who was prime minister of Britain at the time of the treaty? _____
_____

3 Name two of the Irish team at the treaty discussions in London. _____
_____

4 Name two of the British team at the treaty discussions. _____
_____

5 What caused the civil war? _____
_____

6 How and where did Michael Collins die? _____
_____

■ PEN PORTRAITS OF IRISH LEADERS

Arthur Griffith

- Imprisoned by the British
- Released in 1917
- Set up Sinn Féin party again
- Member of the first government
- Went to London to take part in treaty discussions with the British
- He wanted to win independence peacefully
- Died in August 1922

Arthur Griffith

Michael Collins

- Member of Sinn Féin
- A brave and clever soldier
- Member of the first government
- He believed Volunteers would have to fight for peace
- Killed in an ambush, 22 August 1922

Michael Collins

Éamon de Valera

- Born in New York
- Reared by his mother's family in Bruree in Co. Limerick
- Graduated from university and became a mathematics teacher
- Involved in the Gaelic League, the Irish Volunteers, and the IRB
- After 1916 did not support the IRB
- Sentenced to death for his part in the 1916 rising, but sentence commuted to life imprisonment due to American citizenship

Éamon de Valera

■ IMPORTANT DATES

- 1884   GAA founded
- 1891   Death of Parnell
- 1893   Foundation of the Gaelic League
- 1905   Foundation of Sinn Féin
- 1912   Formation of Ulster Volunteers
- 1913   Irish Citizen Army founded
- 1913   Irish Volunteers founded
- 1916   Easter Rising
- 1917   De Valera elected president of Sinn Féin
- 1919   De Valera elected president of Dáil
- 1919-1921   War of Independence
- 1922   Civil war begins; death of Griffith and Collins

Put words from the box in the spaces.

war	Griffith	surrendered	1918	de Valera
twenty-six	1921	MacSwiney	heroes	truce
Dáil	Collins	independence	six	

When the First World War ended in the year _____ , a general election was held in Britain and Ireland. The majority of MPs elected in Ireland wanted Irish _____.

They decided to set up a parliament in Dublin called the _____. The president of the Dáil was Éamon ___ _____ , even though he was still in prison. Open warfare broke out between Britain and the Irish republicans. De Valera and Michael Collins became Irish _____. The death of Terence _____, Lord Mayor of Cork, focused the attention of the world on the Irish struggle.

A reign of terror raged from 1919 - _____. In 1921 a _____ was arranged. The Irish delegation that went to London to sign the treaty was led by Michael _____ and Arthur _____. Under the terms of the treaty _____ of the counties in Ulster would remain within the United Kingdom and the other _____ counties were to be known as the Irish Free State.

Not all the Irish were happy with the treaty and they began to fight among themselves. Civil _____ broke out and lasted until 1923, when the anti-treaty forces _____.

■ WORD SEARCH

C	O	N	N	O	L	L	Y	C	I	V
A	I	G	L	W	A	R	E	S	T	L
S	A	R	R	T	E	D	A	W	H	A
E	P	E	A	R	S	E	T	D	E	R
M	N	G	T	H	C	U	S	A	C	K
E	E	O	D	Á	I	L	D	V	I	I
N	S	R	A	G	R	E	E	I	D	N
T	O	Y	N	T	H	E	T	T	R	E
A	T	G	R	I	F	F	I	T	H	Y

There are eight names hidden in this word puzzle. The clues will
help you to identify them. Find them and cross them out. The
remaining letters, in order, reveal a hidden statement. Write out
the statement.

1 He was a trade union leader.
2 He founded the Citizen Army.
3 He wrote *The Lake Isle of Inisfree*.
4 He founded the GAA.
5 He was arrested near Tralee Bay.
6 She helped to found the Abbey Theatre.
7 He founded the Land League.
8 He read the proclamation outside the GPO in 1916.
9 He founded Sinn Féin.

Hidden statement:

_____

_____

MODERN IRELAND

■ FACT FILE

The new state

The Dáil met in Leinster House for the first time in 1922. It has been meeting there ever since.

Leinster House

A constitution was drafted:

1 The parliament was to consist of two houses, the Dáil and the Senate.
2 A member of the Dáil was to be known as a Teachta Dála (TD).
3 Election to Dáil and Senate was to be by proportional representation.

The ruling party in the new Dáil consisted of the TDs who were in favour of accepting the treaty. They formed a new party called **Cumann na nGaedheal**, and its president was **William T. Cosgrave**, who was also head of government.

William T. Cosgrave

The civil service, which was inherited from the British government, was reorganised.

The new police force, the Garda Síochána, was to be unarmed.

Members of the Garda Síochána marching into Dublin Castle

A new army was recruited.

The new court system was based on the British system which had been in force before independence.

The Irish language was given greater importance in the education system.

■ EXERCISES

Imagine that your county has gained independence from the rest of the country and you have been elected president.

1 Give your new country a name.
2 List five things which must be attended to at once.

■ FACT FILE

In 1926 de Valera left Sinn Féin because he disagreed with its policy of boycotting elections to the Dáil. He formed a new party, **Fianna Fáil**.

The 1927 election returned the following numbers of TDs:

Cumann na nGaedheal	47
Fianna Fáil	44
Labour	22
Others	40

Fianna Fáil refused to take their seats in the Dáil because members were obliged to take an oath of allegiance to the king of England.

Kevin O'Higgins, the new Minister for Justice and External Affairs, was assassinated in 1927. As a result the government brought in a Public Safety Act, forbidding the bearing of arms. They also passed a law compelling those seeking election to take an oath promising to take their seats if elected.

Kevin O'Higgins

So de Valera and Fianna Fáil entered the Dáil. They took the oath of allegiance to the king of England, but stated formally that the oath had no meaning for them.

In 1927, de Valera and members of Fianna Fáil enter the Dáil for the first time

The ESB was established and an electricity-generating station was built on the Shannon, just above Limerick.

Electricity-generating station on the Shannon. Opened 1929

In 1932 a Fianna Fáil government came to power after the election. They released IRA prisoners, who had been imprisoned by the Cumann na nGaedheal government. The IRA then began to disrupt Cumann na nGaedheal meetings.

Some former army officers formed an organisation called the Army Comrades Association to protect political meetings from being attacked by the IRA. They wore a kind of uniform consisting of blue shirt and black beret, and they became known as the **Blueshirts**.

The Blueshirts

The IRA became weaker as many of its members joined Fianna Fáil. The Blueshirts, too, broke up, but they joined with Cumann na nGaedheal and the Farmers' Party to form **Fine Gael**.

The economic war

The Fianna Fáil government withheld annuity payments to the British government. The annuities were for repayment of loans which the British government made to Irish farmers to help them buy their land. The British retaliated by putting a tax of 20% on Irish cattle imports. The Irish government then taxed some British goods and the 'economic war' had begun. It caused great hardship in Ireland, especially to farmers.

In 1938 de Valera and the British prime minister, Neville Chamberlain, reached an agreement that ended the economic war. In return for a payment of £10 million, Britain gave up the claim to the land annuities, and normal trading between the two countries was resumed. In addition, Britain returned to the Irish Free State some ports which they had retained under the treaty of 1922.

A new constitution

In 1937 de Valera offered the country a new constitution. A Dáil election was fought on it and Fianna Fáil won. The constitution was formally adopted by the Dáil. That constitution (**Bunreacht na hÉireann**) is still in place.

Under the constitution the new head of state was to be a president elected for a period of seven years. The first president was Dr. Douglas Hyde, founder of the Gaelic League. The title of the head of government was changed to Taoiseach and the deputy to Tánaiste. The state was to be called Éire.

■ EXERCISE

The constitution may be changed only by a referendum.
Has this been done? What changes have been made?
Write your answers.

■ FACT FILE

The Second World War began on 1 September 1939.

Ireland took a neutral position in the war and became semi-isolated. It was difficult to provide the necessities of life for the people, and rationing of some foods, clothing, coal, and petrol was introduced.

In the first election after the war (1948) Fianna Fáil failed to win an over-all majority, and the first coalition government was formed consisting of Fine Gael, Labour, Clann na Talmhan, and a new party, Clann na Poblachta. **John A. Costello** was Taoiseach.

The new government declared Ireland a republic in 1949. Its name was changed to **Republic of Ireland**, the name it has today.

John A. Costello

The Republic of Ireland since 1949

In 1955 Ireland joined the United Nations.

Ireland in the 1950s had massive unemployment and emigration. In 1959 de Valera retired from the Dáil and was elected to the presidency. **Seán Lemass** became Taoiseach. His new economic policies brought great improvements and prosperity in the 1960s.

Since Lemass Ireland has had six Taoisigh:

- Jack Lynch
- Liam Cosgrave
- Charles Haughey
- Garret FitzGerald
- Albert Reynolds
- John Bruton

Seán Lemass cycling to work during the war years to encourage saving petrol for essential transport

In 1960 Irish soldiers were first sent out on a peace-keeping mission for the United Nations Organisation (UNO). They went to the Belgian Congo (Zaire). They have been in many countries since then on similar missions.

■ GLEANINGS

Funeral of Irish soldiers killed in the Congo while serving for the UNO

(a) What do you call the soldiers marching beside the coffins?
(b) What are resting on the coffins?
(c) Why, do you think, did so many people turn out for the funeral?

■ FACT FILE

1961 RTE was established to broadcast television in Ireland.

1967 Free post-primary education for all children was granted.

1968 The civil rights movement began in Northern Ireland. The nationalist minority protested against discrimination, especially in the giving of houses and jobs. 25 years of violence, murder and bombing followed.

1972 The Northern Ireland parliament was removed and the province has since been ruled directly by the British parliament in London.

Several attempts have been made by the British and Irish governments to solve the problem of Northern Ireland, but so far they have not been successful.

1973 Ireland joined the European Economic Community (EEC).

1990 Mary Robinson was elected seventh president of Ireland. She is the first woman to hold this office. Her predecessors were

- Douglas Hyde
- Seán T. O'Kelly
- Éamon de Valera
- Erskine Childers
- Cearbhall Ó Dálaigh
- Patrick Hillery.

■ EXERCISE

Write five sentences about any one of the people pictured below.

_____

_____

_____

_____

_____

_____

_____

_____

_____

TEST YOURSELF QUIZ 3

1 Who was first leader of the Irish Free State?
2 What was W.T. Cosgrave's party?
3 Who set up the Fianna Fáil party?
4 What year was the new constitution written?
5 When did the Second World War begin?
6 How many years did the Second World War last?
7 Who headed the first coalition government in Ireland?
8 Who brought in economic policies that improved the prosperity of the country in the 1960s?
9 How many Taoisigh have we had since Séan Lemass?
10 What do the letters EEC stand for?
11 In what year did Ireland join the EEC?
12 Name three other countries that are now members of the European Community.
13 What do the letters UNO stand for?
14 Who was the first president of Ireland? Who is president of our country now?
15 When was Séan Lemass appointed Taoiseach?
16 Name some items that were rationed during the Second World War.
17 Who became Taoiseach after the 1948 election?
18 In what year was Ireland declared a republic?
19 Ireland's peace-keeping soldiers first went to the Belgian Congo. What is that country now called?
20 Who succeeded de Valera as president of Ireland?
21 What reforms were sought by the civil rights movement in Northern Ireland?
22 When was the Northern Ireland parliament suspended?
23 The EEC has become the EC. What did the letter now omitted stand for?
24 Who became president of Ireland in 1990?

Acknowledgements

The publishers wish to thank the following for assistance with photographic material and for permission to reproduce photographs in this book:

Bulloz, Paris; ESB Archives, Dublin; Hulton Deutsch Collection, London; Lensmen and Assoc., Dublin; Mansell Collection, London; National Library of Ireland, Dublin; The Office of Public Works, Dublin; Sportsfile, Dublin.

The publishers wish to thank Faber and Faber Ltd., London, for permission to include *Requiem for the Croppies* from DOOR INTO THE DARK by Seamus Heaney and extracts from *For the Commander of the Eliza* from DEATH OF A NATURALIST by Seamus Heaney.

Every effort has been made to locate all sources of copyright used in this publication, but a small number remain untraced. On the establishment of such sources the publishers are willing to reach a satisfactory agreement with the holders.